JASMINE TOGUCHI

TOGUCHI

MOCHI QUEEN

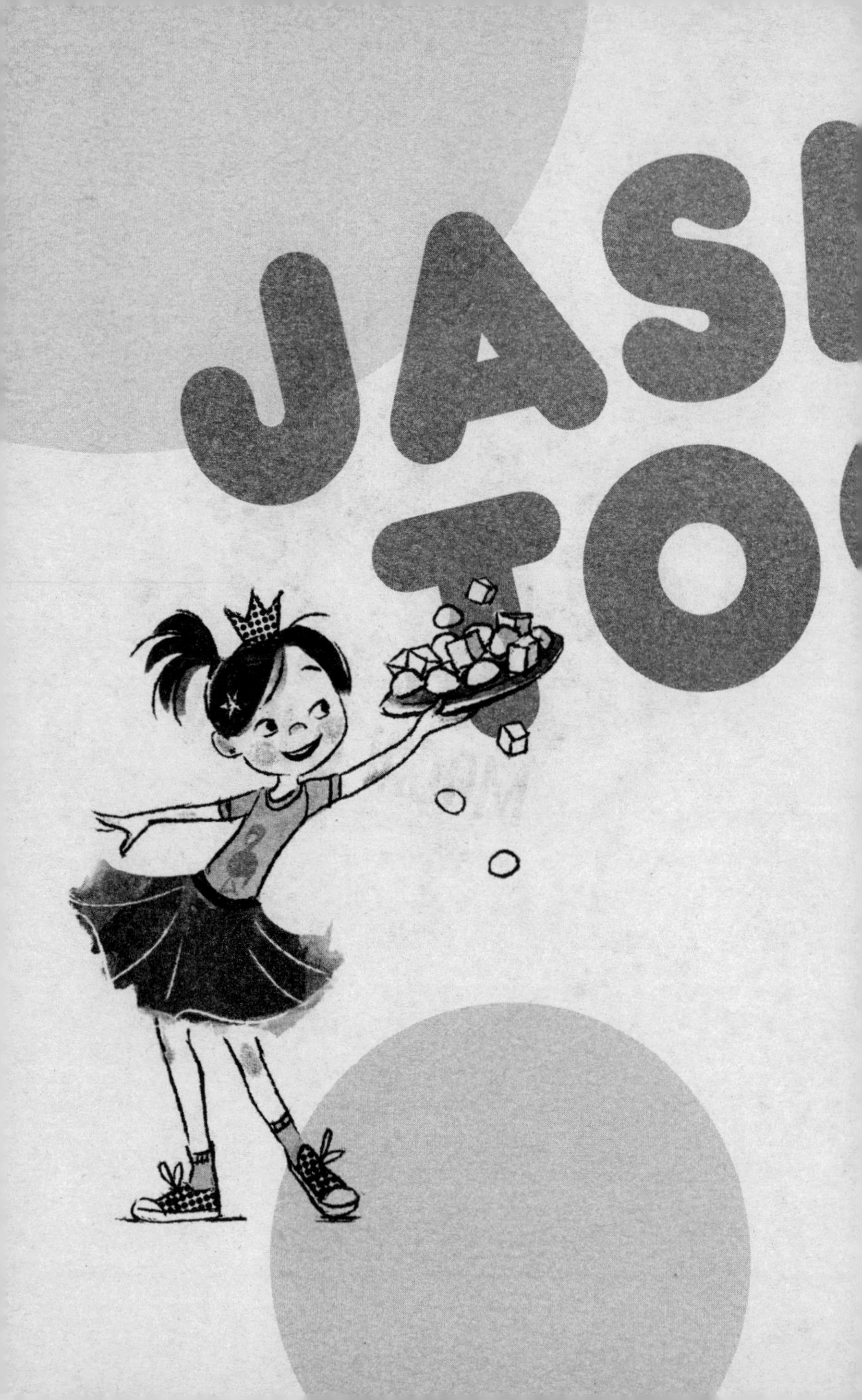

MINE GUCHI

MOCHI QUEEN

DEBBI MICHIKO FLORENCE   PICTURES BY ELIZABET VUKOVIĆ

SCHOLASTIC INC.

ISBN 978-1-338-25525-6

Text copyright © 2017 by Debbi Michiko Florence. Illustrations copyright © 2017 by Elizabet Vuković. All rights reserved. Published by Scholastic Inc., 557 Broadway, New York, NY 10012, by arrangement with Farrar, Straus and Giroux, LLC. SCHOLASTIC and associated logos are trademarks and/or registered trademarks of Scholastic Inc.

12 11 10 9 8 7 6 5 4 3 2 1   17 18 19 20 21 22

Printed in the U.S.A.   40

First Scholastic printing, October 2017

Designed by Kristie Radwilowicz

FOR MY DAUGHTER,
CAITLIN MASAKO SCHUMACHER,
WHO EATS HER MOCHI WITH
CINNAMON AND SUGAR —D.M.F.

FOR ANNA,
MY SISTER AND
BEST FRIEND —E.V.

CONTENTS

JASMINE TOGUCHI

MOCHi QUEEN

A TERRIFIC IDEA

It was safest for me to hide in my room. Mom was scrubbing the guest bathroom. Dad was getting the cardboard boxes from the garage. My big sister, Sophie, was sweeping the kitchen floor. I waited for my chance to escape the cleaning frenzy.

I, Jasmine Toguchi, do *not* like to clean! But I do like to climb trees, eat dessert, and make messes. I'd rather do any of those things right now.

I peeked out my bedroom window. Dad has moved into the backyard! I tiptoed out of my room. Nobody in the hall! I ran to the front door. But just as I put my hand on the doorknob, I heard footsteps behind me.

"Jasmine Toguchi, where do you think you're going?"

I turned slowly to face my mother.

"We need to clean the house before everyone arrives tomorrow," Mom said. "Now go help your sister."

Walnuts! This was *exactly* what I was trying to avoid. Helping Sophie would mean that I did all the work while she bossed me around.

"I already finished sweeping," Sophie announced from the next room. Scattered across the kitchen floor, small mounds of dust and bits of trash sat like sand dunes on the beach. Except this was no vacation. "You can pick it all up. I'll let you know if you do a good job."

Sophie is two years older than me. She thinks that makes her my boss. If that weren't annoying enough, she also gets to do everything before me. She started school first. She learned to read first. She even started piano lessons last year, and I have to wait another year. Not that I really want to play the piano.

Sophie was always the expert. She thought she was smarter and better than me. Just once, I wished I could do something first. Just once, I wanted to be the expert.

As I swept the piles into the dustpan, Sophie climbed up onto the kitchen stool. It was like being higher up made her more in charge. This meant barking commands at me while she picked at the chipped polish on her fingernails.

"You missed a pile!"

"Stop sweeping so hard! You're making dust fly into the air!"

"Don't spill or you'll have to clean it up."

I sighed and swept.

We were getting ready for mochi-tsuki. Every year, our relatives come over to our house to celebrate New Year's. We spend the entire day making mochi, Japanese sweet rice cakes. It's hard work to make mochi, but there's a reward—eating the gooey treat afterward.

Actually, all the other relatives do the hard work. In my family, you had to be at least ten years old to make mochi. This year would be Sophie's first time getting to help. I'm only eight. Once again, Sophie would do something before I did. By the time I was ten and got to make mochi, too, she would be the expert and boss me around. That would take all the fun out of it.

This year, just like last year, I would be stuck babysitting.

I bent over, scooped, and walked to the trash can to empty the dustpan. I did this a hundred times, at least.

I wished I could help with mochi-tsuki. I didn't want

to watch DVDs with my four-year-old cousins. It wasn't fair. I was big enough to make mochi!

"I'm going to help make mochi," I said to Sophie.

She kept picking at her orange nails. "You're too little. You'll only get in the way."

"I'm big enough." Yesterday I noticed I came up to Sophie's chin. During the summer I came up to her shoulder. I was growing!

"Just wait your turn," she said.

This year, Sophie would sit at the table in the backyard with Mom and all the other women. She would probably get to sit right next to Obaachan, our grandma who came from Japan every year for the holidays.

"Stop pouting and finish cleaning," Sophie said. "You'll get your turn at mochi-tsuki when you're ten."

I wished there was something I could do before her. Something she could never do.

I swept up another dust pile. Suddenly, I got

an idea. It was tradition for Dad, the uncles, and the boy cousins to turn the cooked rice into the sticky mochi by pounding it in a stone bowl with a big wooden hammer. That's what I could do. I could pound mochi with the boys!

"What are you grinning about?" Sophie scooted off the stool and took the dustpan from me. "Sweep the floor again to make sure there's nothing left."

You needed to be strong to pound mochi. I was strong. So I swept the floor using all my muscles.

"Stop!" Sophie screeched. "You almost hit me! Mom! Jasmine tried to whack me in the head with the broom!"

Hitting Sophie sounded like good practice for pounding mochi, but I knew it would only get me in trouble.

Just then Mom walked into the kitchen, her forehead wrinkled like it always was when she got annoyed.

"Jasmine Toguchi! You know better than that. Go clean your room if you can't work well with your sister."

I handed the broom to Sophie with a smile and skipped to my room to work on my terrific idea!

MY
THiNKiNG
SPOT

Cleaning my bedroom is easy. Sophie brags that her bedroom is bigger than mine, but I love my room. It is cozy and I always finish cleaning my room before Sophie cleans hers.

The messiest part of my room is usually my desk. It used to be Dad's desk when he was a boy. Sophie's desk came from a store, but I liked that my desk was special. My dad used to do his homework on the same desk I do my projects on now.

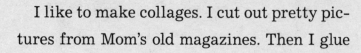

I like to make collages. I cut out pretty pictures from Mom's old magazines. Then I glue the pictures onto a piece of cardboard. One time, though, I cut up Mom's magazine before she was finished reading it. Now we have a deal. When she finishes a magazine, she puts it on my desk. I had a whole mess of magazines.

I was working on a collage of my favorite color, purple. I

scooped up the pile of pictures of grapes and plums and flowers and butterflies and a lavender sunset, and put them into a big envelope. I stacked the magazines into a neat pile. While I did this, I thought about mochitsuki. I not only needed to convince my parents to let me help, but to let me join the boys, too. My mom was all about rules. This was going to be tough.

I needed to go to my thinking spot.

We lived on what Mom called a quiet street, like that was a good thing. That meant there was no one to play with. My best friend, Linnie Green, lived too far for me to walk to see her.

Fortunately Mrs. Reese lived only two houses down. And even though she was old, older than Mom and Dad, she was fun to be around. She listens to me when I talk and doesn't tell me what to do, like *Elbows off the table!* or *Don't make too much noise.* She also let me have a special thinking spot in her backyard.

RULES

1. Use your manners.

2. No feathers in the bathtub!

3. Chopsticks are not for drumming.

I liked going to Mrs. Reese's, especially because Sophie never went there. Mom said as long as I didn't bother Mrs. Reese, I could visit with her.

I am pretty sure I never bothered her.

Mrs. Reese was sitting in a rocking chair on her porch like she usually did after lunch.

"How are you today, Jasmine?" Mrs. Reese asked, putting her book on her lap. She was al-ways reading. "Your mother says your rela-tives are coming. You must be excited!"

Mrs. Reese moved here from Vermont in the summer, so she didn't know about our tradition. She told me it was very cold and snowy there in the winter. Here in Los Angeles we never get snow, and it mostly stays sunny.

"We're getting ready for mochi-tsuki. *Moh-chee-tsoo-kee.*" I pronounced it slowly for her, because she wasn't Japanese-American like me. I couldn't really speak or understand Japanese, but I knew a few words.

She nodded as I sat down on her front steps. "What is that?"

"Every year, our relatives come over to make mochi. It's a Japanese dessert. It's good luck to start the new year by eating mochi." I closed my eyes, imagining biting into the chewy treat.

My favorite holiday is New Year's, when the whole family gets together. My mom likes Christmas best. I like it fine, especially the presents. Sophie's favorite day is her birthday.

"Is it a lot of work to make mochi?" Mrs. Reese asked.

"It takes two days!"

"Two whole days? Wow! What do you do?"

I frowned. Telling Mrs. Reese that I sat and watched TV with my cousins was not interesting. If only *I* could make mochi.

"Dad sets up the backyard with tables and

chairs," I said. "Mom and my grandma wash special rice and then soak it overnight. When the rest of the relatives come over the next day, they cook the rice. The men pound the rice into mochi and the women roll the mochi into little balls."

I just *had* to be able to help make mochi! I needed to think of a way to convince my parents. Good thing I had the perfect thinking spot.

"I'm going to climb your tree now," I said. Mrs. Reese told me I could climb her apricot tree any time I wanted. That was my special place. The only rule was that I couldn't fall out of it.

In her backyard, I climbed to my favorite spot for thinking, in the crook of the bottom branches. I could lean against the tree trunk and not be afraid of falling. Not that I was afraid. I just didn't want to break Mrs. Reese's rule of not falling out.

Most of the leaves were gone by now. I could see my backyard from here. Dad had already set up the canopy to shade the tables. Why did only the men pound mochi? Was it because they were strong? But girls were strong, too.

Last week, Tommy Fraser, a boy in my third-grade class, couldn't open his water bottle and he asked me for help. I opened it for him.

If I could show Dad that I was strong, maybe he would let me join the men.

There was a special hammer they used to pound mochi. I couldn't practice with it yet because it was still packed in a box. I would just have to use my arm muscles as much as possible before the big day. Then finally my muscles would get strong enough to lift the hammer! I wrapped my arms around the tree and hugged it.

I had a plan.

THE PLAN
IN ACTION

When I got home, Sophie was in the kitchen with Mom. She was washing lettuce in the sink while Mom stirred a pot on the stove. My tummy rumbled as I smelled tomato sauce. Mom's spaghetti was the best!

"Can I help?" I asked, hoping I could be Mom's helper, too, like Sophie.

"Thank you, Jasmine," Mom said, "but we've got it."

"Yeah," Sophie said. "Mom and I are busy."

I stayed in the kitchen, thinking that maybe

they would need my help later on.

Mom turned to get something out of the fridge and almost bumped into me.

"Jasmine, why don't you make a collage in your room?"

I slunk into the living room and plopped down on the couch. I didn't want to make a collage right now. I wanted to spend time with Mom, because she wasn't home a lot.

Mom worked part-time as an editor. An editor reads other people's work and fixes the words. Like my teachers. My teachers were always fixing my writing. Part-time meant that Mom worked part of her time away from home and the other part at home. I liked the part when she was home. Especially because when she wasn't home, like on Thursdays, Sophie and I had a babysitter.

Mrs. Peepers was boring. She followed

all of Mom's rules. My best friend Linnie's babysitter was in high school. They baked cookies, did their nails, and watched TV. All good stuff compared to the homework and quiet time Mrs. Peepers made us do.

By the time Mom called us for dinner, I was starving. Dad, Sophie, and I ate with forks, but Mom ate with chopsticks. She liked using chopsticks for eating everything except ice cream and cereal.

I slurped noodle after noodle. I remembered I needed to build up my arm muscles, so I twirled my pasta extra-hard.

"Mom!" Sophie screeched. "Jasmine is splattering spaghetti sauce everywhere!"

"Jasmine Toguchi!" Mom said. "Be careful. The floor is clean."

Sophie smirked, but I ignored her.

After dinner, I said, "I can wash the dishes." I had never washed dishes before, but it couldn't be that hard. You just had to scrub and rinse and lift dishes and pots and pans. All good things for using my arms.

Dad raised his eyebrows. Mom's mouth made a small O. Sophie glared at me.

"How nice of you," Mom said. She gave me her proud smile, the one that made her eyes happy. "I'll wash and you can rinse."

I stood next to Mom at the sink and rinsed dishes. My back started to hurt from standing there for so long, but I didn't complain. I tried to pick up the whole stack of dishes at once to show Mom how strong I was, but she made me rinse one dish at a time.

"I'll get the spaghetti pot," I said, reaching over to the counter.

"I'll get that—" Mom started to say.

My hands were wet and slippery. I pulled the pot off the counter.

Clang! The pot crashed to the floor!

Sophie ran into the kitchen.

"What was that?" she asked, even though it was perfectly clear.

Sophie loved to see me get in trouble. She was disappointed because instead of getting mad, Mom told Sophie we were doing fine.

I looked at my spaghetti-thin arms. That pot was heavy! Was the mochi hammer that heavy? All the spaghetti I had eaten tied into knots in my stomach. Mochi-tsuki was in three days. I had to get strong, fast!

OBAACHAN'S GIFT

The next day, it was time to pick up Obaachan from the airport. Sophie and I ran around the house shouting for joy. Mom ran around the house, too. She fluffed the couch pillows four times. She straightened the painting over the fireplace twice. She dusted the vase Obaachan brought the last time she visited.

Sophie and I went into the bedroom where Obaachan always stayed. Sophie left a note on the nightstand. On the pillow, I put a collage of birds that I had made. Obaachan loved birds. Right in the center of the collage was my very favorite bird in the world. A flamingo! Someday I hoped I could have a pet flamingo.

Mom shooed us out of the room, and then out of the house. She never let us go with her and Dad to the airport. She said we were out of control.

Sophie went to her best friend's house. I stayed at Mrs. Reese's.

Mrs. Reese put a big plate of brownies in front of me. "Your favorite," she said. "No nuts."

I took only one. Mom said I always had to use my manners, especially when I was a guest. Mrs. Reese baked the best brownies, so it was hard not to gobble up all of them. She never ate any brownies, not that I ever saw. Maybe she made them special just for me.

"How go the preparations?" she asked.

"Okay," I said after I swallowed a big chocolaty bite. "My grandma comes today. We call her Obaachan." I sounded it out for Mrs. Reese.

"*Oh-baah-chan*. She and Mom will probably clean the house more."

I didn't understand why they spent so much time cleaning when everything would just get dirty again.

HIROSHIMA

"You must be happy to see your grandma," Mrs. Reese said. "I know I'm excited about seeing my grandson when I visit my daughter tomorrow."

Mrs. Reese's daughter lives in Los Angeles. That's why she moved here from Vermont. I wondered if someday Obaachan might move here. That would be great!

"Where is your grandma coming from?" Mrs. Reese asked.

"Hiroshima. It's a city in Japan. She comes every year and stays for a whole month."

"You said your other relatives visit, too. When do they get here?" Mrs. Reese asked.

Mean cousin Eddie would come tomorrow. He and his parents live in San Francisco and it takes them eight hours to drive here. They would stay overnight at our house. I didn't want to think about mean cousin Eddie.

The rest of the family, with my nice cousins, lives near us in Los Angeles. That's what I was looking forward to.

"Tomorrow and the day after," I answered.

In two days, everyone except for me and my four-year-old cousins would make mochi. I had to get my arms ready.

"Do you have any wood that needs chopping?" I asked.

Mrs. Reese crinkled her forehead. It was the same look Mom made when I asked something she thought was strange.

"Or maybe hammering? Do you have

anything that needs to be hammered?" I glanced around the kitchen. The cabinets looked fine. Too bad.

"The shed needs painting," Mrs. Reese said slowly, like she was thinking of not telling me.

I jumped up, brownie crumbs flying. "I'll do it!"

"Well, it's a job that will take some time and I know your parents will be home soon with your grandma."

I sank back into the kitchen chair. I felt like a balloon with a hole in it.

"My!" Mrs. Reese said with a smile. "You sure want to help out! I'll tell you what, you can help me paint the shed after the holidays. On a weekend."

Oh. I didn't want to help after mochi-tsuki. It would be no use to work out my arms afterward. Besides, painting sounded boring.

Fortunately, before I had to answer, my parents' car pulled into our driveway.

"Thank you for the brownies! I'll see you later," I said, dashing out the door to greet Obaachan.

When I got back to the house, Sophie wasn't home yet. For once, I had Obaachan to myself. I flung myself at her as she stepped out of the car. She smelled like a pine forest. She laughed and patted my cheek.

I leaned back to look at Obaachan. Her short silver hair was like a fluffy cloud around her head. She smiled at me, her brown eyes

crinkling, and my insides felt warm and sweet, like Mrs. Reese's brownies.

Dad carried Obaachan's luggage into the house. She had a lot of stuff! I hoped something in there was a gift for me, but I knew better than to ask.

I followed Obaachan to the guest room.

"Very nice!" she said when she saw my collage on her pillow.

She unpacked her clothes one by one. Black pants. Gray pants. A dark blue dress. A white blouse. A gray sweater. Some clothes she hung in the closet. Others she folded and put in the dresser. She brought out a pretty blue-and-gray kimono that she would wear on New Year's Day. It was my favorite outfit of hers. I sat on a chair and tried to be patient.

After unpacking a million clothes, she

turned to me with a package wrapped in red-and-white cloth. My heart did a happy dance.

"For you, Misa-chan," Obaachan said, calling me by my Japanese middle name.

I made a proper bow and thanked her. "Arigato, Obaachan." I almost snatched the gift out of her hands, but I remembered my manners and took it slowly.

I untied the gold string and the cloth fell away from a box. I lifted the lid. Under gold tissue paper was a white apron decorated with pink cherry blossoms. I pulled it from the box and held it up. It was so pretty! It looked like Mom's special mochi apron, except hers was red with white cherry blossoms. I ran over to the mirror on the closet and draped the apron over my head. It hung to my knees and gaped at my neck. It

was a little big, but I didn't care! I had a special mochi apron!

"Wowee zowee! I love it, Obaachan!" My smile was so big my cheeks hurt.

"Save for when you help with mochi-tsuki," she said.

My smile slumped into a frown. More waiting. I was tired of waiting.

"I'm going to help this year," I announced.

Obaachan's eyes clouded over. "You too young."

Last year, I wanted to decorate the house for Mom's birthday, but I thought I was too little. Obaachan told me I was big enough. We worked together and didn't tell anyone else. We were a team. Obaachan was always on my side.

"But I'm ready to help," I said. "I'm going to pound mochi."

Obaachan gasped. "You young lady! That job for men."

I shook my head. "It doesn't matter," I said, trying to use a respectful tone, like Mom taught me. "I am just as tough as the boys."

"Girls no pound mochi. It kisoku, the rule."

That was a silly rule from when Obaachan was little, probably. Walnuts! Everything had rules! It wasn't fair! I shouldn't have told Obaachan. I didn't want to wait two more years. I didn't want to roll mochi. I wanted to *pound* mochi!

I ran out of the room, leaving the apron behind.

MUSCLES NEEDED

The next morning, Sophie paraded into the kitchen wearing her new apron. Hers was white with blue cherry blossoms and fit perfectly. She marched around the table where I was sitting, pumping her arms like she was the leader of a band.

"You don't need to wear that till tomorrow," I said.

"You're just jealous," she said. She circled me one more time before she sat down at the table.

What happened to my
apron? I wondered
if Obaachan had
packed it away.

Obaachan and
Mom spoke Japanese to
each other as they washed and soaked the
special sweet rice at the sink. I didn't understand what they were saying. I hoped
Obaachan wouldn't tell Mom that I wanted
to pound mochi. Maybe she would keep my
secret. Mom was all about rules, and she might
feel the same way as Obaachan, that girls

weren't strong enough. I realized that I had to have proof that I could pound mochi before I asked my parents.

I stared into my bowl of cereal as I ate, so I wouldn't have to look at Sophie in her new apron. What could I do to prove I had good muscles? I glanced around the kitchen. There wasn't anything heavy to lift.

Last month in school, Sophie had to take a physical education test. She had to pull herself up on a bar. Maybe I could show my parents that I could hang on to a tree branch for a long time. First, I needed to test myself to make sure I could do it.

There was more cleaning after breakfast! It was never-ending. Finally, after lunch I was able to escape. I walked straight to Mrs. Reese's backyard, scrambled over the fence, and climbed into my secret thinking spot.

I rolled up my sleeve and tried to make a muscle. I squinted at my arm. My muscle was smaller than a ladybug. I squeezed my arm tight, but still nothing. It didn't look anything like when Dad bent his arm.

I leaned over and shook the branch, and the few leaves that were left rustled. I slid out onto the branch and gripped it with both hands. I let my body drop. But my hands slipped and I fell onto the grass below. I sat there, blinking quickly. My arms were weaker than spaghetti noodles. Mom and Dad would never believe I could pound mochi.

I wasn't going to give up, though. I climbed back into the tree and rubbed my hands on my T-shirt, drying them off. I crawled over the branch. Then I took a deep breath, made sure I had a good grip, and slowly eased off the branch. I held on tight. I didn't fall!

"Jasmine!" Mom's voice carried into Mrs. Reese's yard.

I hung on to the branch and counted to five.

"Jasmine! Are you out there?"

I counted to ten!

"Jasmine Toguchi!" Mom called again. "Come home right away. Your cousin will be here soon."

I finally let go and dropped down to the grass. I did it! Now I just had to show my parents. If they saw I could hang on to the branch, they'd know I was strong enough to lift the mochi hammer.

If only mean cousin Eddie weren't coming today. Last year, he kept calling me and Sophie babies because we couldn't help with mochi-tsuki. He wouldn't be able to tease Sophie this year.

I would rather eat dirt than spend time with mean cousin Eddie. I would rather take orders from bossy Sophie. I would rather paint

Mrs. Reese's shed. But if I wanted to pound mochi, I had to go home.

I climbed back over the fence. It was much easier this time to lift myself over it. I was definitely strong enough to pound mochi. This year, mean cousin Eddie couldn't tease *me* either!

MEAN COUSIN EDDIE

Dad and Uncle Jimmy unfolded two long tables in the backyard. That was where the women would roll mochi tomorrow. Mom, Obaachan, and Auntie Laurie covered the tables with a green plastic tablecloth. Sophie taped it down.

I watched from the window in the kitchen. The sky was blue and cloudless and the sun was shining, but I didn't feel very sunshiny.

"Well, if it isn't Jasmine T who smells like pee!"

I hunched my shoulders and leaned my chin on my hand. Mean cousin Eddie's voice sounded like yowling cats.

Dad is a professor of history at a college. He teaches about things that have already happened. He says that sometimes history repeats itself. Eddie and I have a repeating history. Every time we get together, he teases me and I get upset. Three years ago, he fell off the couch while he was jumping on it. Maybe he bumped his head super-hard, because after that he got mean. Sophie thought it was because we saw him cry.

"Everyone else is helping, but not you," mean cousin Eddie said. "You're a weakling!"

Two years ago, he couldn't help either. Dad told

me not to let Eddie get to me. He always told me to count to ten before talking with Eddie. So I counted to twenty.

"What? You can't even turn around? Are you so dumb you can't make conversation?"

The kitchen table scraped against the floor as Eddie bumped into it. I kept staring out the window. I counted to twenty-five.

"You're so lame!"

I counted to thirty.

Finally, Eddie gave up and pushed open the back door. A cool breeze drifted in. It smelled like dry leaves. Outside, Dad and Uncle Jimmy carried the usu from the garage. I stood on my tiptoes to get a better look at the stone bowl they used to turn cooked rice into mochi.

It took two grown men to carry the bowl into the yard. Mean cousin Eddie walked behind them, the wooden hammer on his shoulder, like he was some superstar. When he bent

to put it down, he wobbled like he was about to fall over. I smiled as he struggled. Then I realized that Eddie, who was eleven years old, had trouble lifting the hammer. Maybe hanging down from a tree branch wasn't good enough. Maybe I should make sure I could pick up the hammer.

* * *

I waited until after dinner when everyone was busy watching TV and talking. Sophie was on the phone with her best friend, Maya Fung. Eddie was playing a computer game.

I slowly opened the back door, stopping just before the hinges made their tattletale squeak. I squeezed outside and pulled the door shut behind me with a soft *click*. The pavement felt cold against my bare feet. I had left my shoes behind so I could stay quiet.

Keeping the porch light off so nobody would

see me, I took tiny steps in the dark. I put my hands on the mochi table and followed it around to the edge of the yard. There, the usu and hammer were covered with a tarp.

I could just barely see them, looking like a creature standing guard. I shivered and glanced back at the house. All quiet.

When I made it to the usu, I slid the tarp off. The mochi hammer shimmered under the stars. I reached over and put my hands around the wooden handle. It felt smooth from all the years of my family's hands gripping it. My heart pounded in my throat. I took big gulping breaths of the cool air.

This was it. If I could pick up the hammer, it meant I was strong enough to pound mochi.

Just as I was about to try lifting it, an all-too-familiar, too-horrible voice sounded from the darkness behind me.

"Hey! What do you think you're doing? You're not allowed to touch that!"

Eddie grabbed the other end of the hammer. We tugged back and forth. I gripped it tightly, refusing to let go. This was a test! If I could just hold on . . .

But Eddie was bigger than me. He yanked the hammer out of my hands and I fell backward. The damp grass soaked into my shorts. Mean cousin Eddie's teeth glowed in the moonlight as he smiled evilly.

"You're so weak," he said.

"I'm not! I can hang from a tree branch."

"So what? Anyone can do that. It doesn't mean anything."

I ran my hand along my arm, feeling for a muscle. Nothing.

"Don't touch this again," he said. "You're a girl. You'll give it bad luck!"

I sucked on my bottom lip. If anything, *he* would give it bad luck with all his meanness.

He stood there staring down at me, trying to scare me. When I didn't budge, he shrugged. I hoped he would leave the hammer, but he took it into the house.

Walnuts! Now what was I going to do?

WANTED: MOCHI HAMMER

When I got back in the house, I planned to look for the hammer.

"Bedtime, Jasmine," Mom said.

"But everyone else is staying up," I said. I had to find that hammer.

"You know the rules."

My bedtime was eight o'clock, but Sophie got to stay up till eight-thirty. Eddie probably didn't have a bedtime. I slouched into my room to get ready for bed. Because we had company, Mom didn't check on me. I brushed my teeth and put on my pajamas in slow-motion. A burst of laughter came from the living room. I straightened up my desk, even though it was neat.

"It's your bedtime, Sophie," I heard Mom say.

I went to my door and peered into the hall. Sophie sat slumped in front of her bedroom. Mom stood there with her arms crossed.

"My night-light is broken. Can I keep the light on?" Sophie asked.

"You know the rules," Mom said.

No lights left on at night. That's one rule that didn't bother me.

"I can't sleep in the dark," Sophie said.

"We don't have any extra night-light bulbs. I'm sorry, sweetheart." Mom walked back to the living room, and Sophie stayed in the hall. If she didn't go to bed soon, she would get in trouble. It would serve her right for being so bossy to me.

Maybe she wouldn't be allowed to make mochi. That would make her sad. But that didn't make me feel happy. I went back into my room and dug around in my closet. I found what I was looking for.

"Here's a flashlight," I said as I handed it to Sophie. "Mom doesn't have a rule about flashlights."

Sophie took it from me slowly, like she thought I might yank it away. As I walked back to my room, I heard her say quietly, "Thanks."

I climbed into bed. I left the curtains open because I liked to see the moon. Sophie was scared of the dark, but not me. I was fearless. That made me smile. I wouldn't let mean cousin Eddie scare me. I would find that hammer first thing in the morning.

* * *

I was already awake when the sun came up. Mom and Dad sleepily stumbled into the hall, mumbling and grumbling. I rolled out of bed with a *thump*, onto my bedroom floor. I had to find that hammer! I got dressed as quickly as I could.

In the kitchen, the rice cookers set on timers were already steaming, filling the kitchen with the smell of rice. My mouth watered. I'd have to wait until midnight before I tasted our mochi. It was the one night of the year I was allowed to stay up past my bedtime. Another reason I loved New Year's.

Obaachan and Mom ate grilled sardines and rice for their breakfast. I didn't want to eat anything that had eyes staring back at me. Dad and Sophie ate oatmeal. Eddie looked like he was still sleeping as he spooned Frosted-Os into his mouth. Most of the cereal just dribbled back into his bowl. *Blech!*

Dad smiled at me. "Good morning. Happy mochi-tsuki day!"

Happy for him and everyone else, maybe.

I wondered where Eddie had hidden the mochi hammer. Maybe I could look for it while everyone was busy eating. I shoved toast into my mouth and gulped my orange juice. Nobody noticed me slip away from the table.

First, I went to Dad's home office, where mean cousin Eddie, Uncle Jimmy, and Auntie Laurie were staying. I looked under the futon. I looked in the closet. I even peeked in Eddie's backpack, but the hammer wasn't anywhere in the room.

Next, I searched the bathroom. It wasn't in the tub or the linen closet. Then I checked Sophie's room. We used to play together there all the time with an awesome dollhouse she got from Obaachan. After she started fifth grade,

though, she said she was too old to play with dolls. I didn't look too hard, because if Sophie caught me in her room, bad things would happen.

I was pretty sure Eddie hadn't hidden it in my parents' room. The only place left to check was Obaachan's room.

I flipped on the light in her room, and my heart lifted when I saw my apron, folded neatly on the desk.

"Misa-chan?" Obaachan said behind me. "You looking for something?"

She followed my gaze. "You want your apron?"

Even though I did, I wanted something else more.

"Eddie took the mochi hammer."

Obaachan frowned. "He say you want to hide it. He give to me."

I was so mad, it felt like my head was full of boiled rice and steam was blowing out of my ears. "That's not true!"

Obaachan sat on her bed and patted the space next to her. I climbed up and she put a gentle hand on my arm.

"I know you sad right now, but your turn come soon. I be very happy when you sit next to me and we roll mochi together."

I liked the idea of sitting with Obaachan, but I didn't want to roll mochi, not even in two years. What I wanted, right now, was to pound mochi with Dad and the uncles. If I could just explain to Obaachan about wanting to do something different from Sophie, she might understand.

But then the doorbell rang. Everyone was here! Obaachan took my hand. Together we walked out to greet the rest of the family. I left behind my apron. Way worse, I left behind the hammer, wherever it was.

THE BiG QUESTION

Auntie Vicky, Uncle Joe, cousins Anna and the twins, Cassie and Leo, walked in. Cassie ran to me the minute she saw me. Her smile made my heart happy again. Uncle Ray, Auntie Beth, and my cousins Jason and Frankie followed.

All around me uncles and aunties and cousins greeted one another. The chattering sounded like a hundred hummingbirds buzzing in the room. Aunties carried in rice cookers and grocery bags. Uncles slapped one another on their backs and talked about football scores.

The four-year-old twins dragged their backpacks over to me. The bags were so full they looked like they were about to explode. Anna ruffled my hair as she walked past. Jason and Frankie ran to find Eddie. My heart felt as

full as the room. I loved being surrounded by my family.

I helped Cassie and Leo unpack stuffed animals and cars and books and crayons. The aunties bustled into the kitchen. By the time the backpacks were empty, so was the living room. I was alone with Cassie and Leo.

Last year, it was me and Sophie together. We built a fort out of the couch cushions. We threw stuffed animals at Eddie any time he walked by. That was fun. Now everyone else was having fun, preparing for mochi-tsuki, without me.

"Play with us," Cassie said as she flopped onto my lap. She was getting heavy!

I had an idea. Cassie had to be heavier than the mochi hammer. I stood up and wrapped my arms around her. I lifted her off the floor and put her down again. She clapped her hands. Leo wanted a turn, too. I lifted him and put him down.

"Again!" Cassie lifted her arms.

"No," Leo said. "My turn."

They pressed against me. I picked Cassie up again. Then I gave Leo another turn, pretending they were mochi hammers. They giggled. I did, too. Now I knew for sure I could lift the mochi hammer. I was ready!

The back door opened. My dad's laughter boomed through the house. I got up and met him in the hallway.

"Hi, Dad," I said. My heart was beating so hard I thought he might be able to hear it.

"My Jasmine!" Dad flashed me a big smile. "How goes the babysitting?"

I caught my bottom lip with my teeth.

Dad looked like he was in a hurry, but when he saw my face he stopped. "What's wrong?"

"I'm afraid to ask you something."

Dad knelt down. "You should never be afraid to talk to me, Jasmine."

"I want to help with mochi-tsuki this year."

Dad waited for me to go on.

"I know the rules say I have to wait until I'm ten, but I think I'm ready."

Dad nodded slowly.

"But," I said, before he told me to talk to Mom, "I don't want to make mochi with Obaachan, Mom, and the aunties."

Dad's lips made a funny sideways move, almost like he was trying not to smile. "No?" he asked. "What do you want to do?"

"I want to pound mochi with you, Dad," I said quickly, so he couldn't tell me no right away. "I've been using my arm muscles a lot to practice, and I know I can lift the hammer. Sophie can be Mom's helper, and I can be yours."

Except I didn't want to help him. I wanted to do it on my own. But sometimes with parents you have to make them feel important.

Dad nodded. "Let me think about it, okay? I'll let you know."

I ran back to Cassie and Leo, full of hope.

THE
LONG
WAIT

The house smelled sweet and the air felt wet. My aunties laughed and chattered in the kitchen. Metal bowls clanked against one another. The women carried big bowls filled with hot rice from the kitchen out to the backyard.

Dad still hadn't come back to tell me I could help. Mochi-tsuki would start very soon, now that the rice was made. I hopped around the room, full of nerves and energy. Waiting was hard!

I played catch with my cousins. They giggled like they were the happiest people on earth. They were definitely the happiest people in this room.

Mean cousin Eddie walked into the living room, brushing his hands off like he'd done something important. He had probably only washed his hands after using the bathroom. At least, I hoped he washed his hands.

"I see you're with the babies, where you be-long," he said.

I didn't remember to count to ten. "In a minute, I'll be outside doing your job for you," I said.

Eddie's mouth gaped open like Mom's break-fast sardine. Then he bent over, laughing.

"You wish!" he said with a snort. "Only men can pound mochi! You're a weakling. When you're ten, you'll be in the kitchen with your sister."

The ball popped out of Cassie's hands and rolled over to Eddie. He nudged it toward me with his foot.

"See ya, Jasmine Pee!"

I forgot to count to ten again. My foot flew out from under me and kicked the ball. *Smack!* It pounded Eddie in the back.

He didn't get a chance to yell at me because Mom beat him to it. "Jasmine Toguchi! What are you doing?"

"Getting the ball for the twins," I said. I

leaned over to pick it up. Eddie cocked his head at me with his eyes narrowed. I waited for him to say something mean, but instead, he went back outside.

Mom nodded at me. "Good job, Jasmine."

But I wasn't doing a good job. I wasn't doing the job I wanted to do at all.

Where was Dad with his answer?

Suddenly, I heard the hammer smack against stone. Oh no! Mochi-tsuki had started without me!

I tossed the ball with Cassie and Leo, back and forth. I wished and wished Dad would come back in to tell me I could help. But instead of Dad, Uncle Jimmy walked in.

"Eddie tells me you want to pound mochi," Uncle Jimmy said.

My insides puffed up with hope.

"You know that it's our family tradition for the boys to pound mochi and the girls to roll," Uncle Jimmy said with a kind smile. "We've been doing it like this since I was a boy."

All the hope leaked out of me.

"But I know how you feel," Uncle Jimmy said. "I'm younger than your dad. I had to wait three whole years before I could help. It felt terrible to watch him pound mochi when I couldn't."

If he was trying to make me feel better, it wasn't working.

"I was glad I waited, though," Uncle Jimmy went on, "because I don't think I would have been much help. Sometimes waiting makes the thing you're waiting for more special."

I had already waited eight years. That was a long time. And I've been waiting forever for Dad to tell me his answer.

"Besides, when you're ten, you'll be happy making mochi with your big sister," Uncle

Jimmy said. "Maybe you can bring the twins outside to watch right now?"

That seemed like the worst idea in the world. Why would I want to watch people doing the thing I most wanted to do?

Dad came into the room. "So, Jasmine," he said, "tell me why you should be allowed to pound mochi."

I stood tall. "Because I'm a bigger girl than people think. I follow directions. Like when Mom tells me to clean my room." I didn't tell Dad about how I didn't do a good job helping Sophie sweep.

Dad nodded.

"And I'm helpful! I'm going to help Mrs. Reese paint her shed." I would definitely do that if it meant I could pound mochi.

"It's hard work, Jasmine," Uncle Jimmy said.

I ran over to Cassie and lifted her up. "I'm strong!"

Leo shouted, "Jasmine's super-strong!"

Cassie wiggled and slipped out of my grip
and landed with a *thunk* on the floor. Thank-
fully, she laughed.

Dad and Uncle Jimmy looked at me. Then
they looked at each other. "Jim," Dad said,
"maybe it's time to break tradition."

Uncle Jimmy smiled and nodded.

"You can pound mochi," Dad said to me.

I felt like shouting and jumping! Instead, I wrapped my arms around Dad's legs and squeezed. "Thank you!"

Dad hugged me and said, "Wow! You really do have strong arms!"

That made me feel even stronger.

This was it! I was getting my wish!

BREAKING
THE RULES

Uncle Jimmy was right about one thing. When you wait and wait for something, it really is wonderful when you get it!

At least, that's how I felt as I walked outside with Dad and Uncle Jimmy. Uncle Ray carried his freshly pounded mochi over to the women.

"Jasmine Toguchi!" Mom said from the table. "What are you doing out here?"

Dad walked over to talk with Mom. Mom's forehead wrinkled.

I wished I could hear what they were saying. I watched for clues. Dad was smiling, and while Mom wasn't exactly smiling, she didn't look mad either. When Mom glanced at me, I straightened my shoulders.

I held my breath as I waited for a sign. Finally, just when I thought my lungs would explode, Mom nodded and I let my breath out in a *whoosh*.

She turned and spoke to the aunties and Obaachan. Everyone at the mochi table looked over at me. Auntie Laurie gave me a thumbs-up. Sophie stuck her tongue out.

This was the first time ever I was breaking a rule! Well, maybe not the first time. I wasn't supposed to watch TV before I finished my homework. I only did that once. Or maybe twice. I did eventually get my homework done, though. I wasn't supposed to eat cookies before dinner. But I only did that a few times.

Okay, so maybe this wasn't the first time I was breaking a rule, but this was the first time I was breaking a rule with Mom and Dad's permission! It felt great!

Cousin Anna waved to me as she went inside. She was going to watch the twins until after I got my turn.

Uncle Jimmy stepped up to the usu with the hammer over his shoulder. Steam from the cooked rice drifted up into the air. Uncle Jimmy gripped the hammer with both hands and swung it down onto the rice.

Thwack! Thwack! Thwack!

He smacked the hammer into the big stone bowl.

Thwack! Thwack! Thwack!

The steamed rice became a lumpy, bumpy blob.

After Uncle Jimmy hit the mochi three times, Uncle Ray reached into the usu to turn the mochi to keep it from sticking to the bowl. Uncle Jimmy hit the mochi again. Uncle Ray dipped his hands into a bowl of water before spinning the mochi another time.

Thwack! Thwack! Thwack! Flip. *Thwack! Thwack! Thwack!* Flip.

Did anyone ever get hit by the hammer? I glanced at Eddie, who stood far away from me. He pretended I wasn't there.

I watched Uncle Jimmy and Uncle Ray pound and flip, flip and pound. It was taking forever. I sat down.

Over at the table, Mom and Obaachan pulled pieces off the giant ball of mochi and passed

them down to my aunties and cousins. Mochiko, rice flour, was sprinkled across the
table like snow so the mochi wouldn't stick to
the tablecloth.

Sophie's hands were white with the rice
flour as she took her piece of mochi and rolled
it between her hands. When it was round like
a ball, she flattened it a little with her palms
and placed it on a big tray.

Sophie was already doing her job. When would I get to do mine?

Both the uncles finally stopped pounding. While Uncle Jimmy took the big lump of mochi over to Mom, Eddie picked up the hammer.

He rested it on his shoulder until Uncle Jimmy came back and stood next to the usu. Dad dumped a glob of rice into the stone bowl.

I paid close attention as Eddie lifted the hammer and dropped it onto the rice.

Thwack!

Eddie pounded the rice two more times.

Thwack!

Thwack!

Uncle Jimmy flipped the mochi. When his hand was safely out of the way, he nodded to Eddie.

Thwack!

Flip.

Eddie swung the hammer easily, but he pounded slower than the uncles. After his dad flipped the ball of rice again, Eddie raised the hammer like he was tired.

A seed of worry formed in my tummy.

Thwack!

Flip.

Thwack!

Flip.

Thwack!

Flip.

Uncle Jimmy took the hammer from Eddie. He patted Eddie on the back and congratulated him. "Great job, son!"

The seed of worry blossomed into a huge flower of worry. That was a good job? Eddie only hit the mochi maybe seven times!

Eddie smiled. Wow. So that's what his face looked like when he was happy.

His face went back to his usual scowl when Dad tapped my shoulder and said, "Your turn, Jasmine!"

MY TURN!

Suddenly, the worry flower in my tummy grew roots all the way down my legs, through my feet, and into the ground. Dad nudged me, but I couldn't move.

"Are you okay?" he asked me.

I nodded, though my feet stayed still.

"Do you want to wait till next year?"

I shook my head. Eddie's smile grew and grew. It wasn't a happy smile or a nice smile. It was a smile that said he was glad I was frozen.

I didn't want to look like a failure. I ripped

my feet from the ground. I moved slowly toward the usu. I took one step after another until I was standing right in front of the bowl. It looked like a giant volcano. It was a lot bigger than I remembered from last night.

The rice Eddie had been pounding still sat in the center of the stone bowl, not yet mochi, but not steamed rice anymore either.

"Are you ready, Jasmine?" Uncle Jimmy asked. "You have to pound the rice while it's hot."

It felt like a huge piece of mochi was stuck in my throat. I swallowed twice before wrapping my hands around the hammer. I glanced over at Mom. Everyone under the canopy stopped working to watch me.

Gulp.

The handle felt slippery. It was hard to get a grip on it.

"Hurry up!" Eddie huffed at me. He dipped his hands into the water, flipped the mochi, and stepped back.

I took a deep breath and gathered all my strength to lift the hammer over my shoulder. I guess I was stronger than I thought because when I swung it back, it kept going. And so did I.

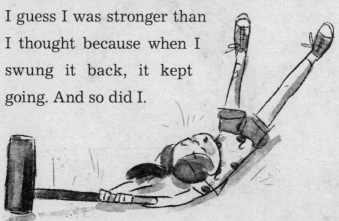

I fell onto the grass. Mean cousin Eddie laughed.

My nose tickled and I blinked quickly.

"Ha! That was hilarious!" Eddie shouted, slapping his knees.

"Eddie!" Uncle Jimmy's voice was sharp. It cut Eddie's laughter off.

I stood and picked up the hammer again. I tried to lift it, but my arms shook, making the hammer wobble.

Eddie snickered, but he kept it low so Uncle Jimmy wouldn't hear.

Dad came up to me. "Do you need help?"

I shook my head.

Suddenly, Sophie was by my side. I was afraid she would laugh at me, too.

But she wasn't laughing. She was glaring at Eddie.

"You can do it, Jasmine," she said. "Remember when you carried Dad's birthday cake all by yourself?"

I was so surprised, I almost fell over a second time.

Her words hugged me. If Sophie believed in me, then I knew I could do it!

I grabbed the hammer tight and lifted it up, but not too high. I let it fall forward.

Thwick.

It only made a tiny sound, but I had hit the rice!

Everyone except for Eddie clapped and cheered. I grinned.

Eddie silently dipped his hands into the water bowl, then flipped the mochi.

I tried but could not lift the hammer again. It felt as heavy as a thousand stones.

Dad came up behind me and wrapped his hands around mine. His hands were warm against my cold skin. I breathed in the peppermint smell of his favorite gum.

"You can do it," Dad whispered as, together, we lifted and dropped the hammer.

Thwack!

Eddie flipped the mochi.

Dad and I hit the mochi again.

Thwack!

I wasn't pounding the mochi by myself.

Thwack!

I was a weakling.

Dad took the hammer from me.

"Fantastic, Jasmine!"

Not fantastic. I only hit the mochi once by myself and it was hardly a real hit. Dad had to help me.

I didn't pound mochi at all! I failed! I failed in front of everyone!

I ran out of the backyard.

RUN AWAY

I ran through the house. I passed cousin Anna, who was still watching the twins. I yanked open the front door. My feet pounded against the concrete as the breeze blew the hair off my face. When I got to Mrs. Reese's yard, I scrambled over the gate and ran to my tree. I leaped for it and climbed up.

I climbed higher than ever. If I looked, I would be able to see into my yard. But the last thing I wanted to see was mochi-tsuki going on without me. So I looked the other way. Just boring black rooftops. I scanned the blue sky, but there weren't any birds or clouds to watch.

I wondered what everyone was doing. Eddie was definitely laughing at me. Dad was probably sorry he let me help. Even though she had been nice to me, I bet Sophie was shaking her head. And Mom was probably ready to yell at me. *Jasmine Toguchi!* she'd say. *What made you think you could help with mochi-tsuki?*

I rubbed my arms. Lifting that hammer was a lot harder than I had thought it would be.

"Hey." Sophie stood at the bottom of my tree.

I didn't answer.

"Everyone is looking for you," she said. Rice flour streaked her hair, making her look a little like Obaachan.

"To yell at me?" I asked.

"No, silly. They think you did a great job."

I squinted down at Sophie, waiting for her joke.

"Was it hard?" Sophie asked, still staring up at me.

I nodded, then climbed back down to talk with her.

"The hammer was heavy," I said.

"But you did it all by yourself."

"Only once. I wasn't strong enough," I said.

Sophie leaned against the tree. "You're strong," she said. "And I'm not talking about muscles. You believe in something and you don't let anyone change your mind."

I looked at my sister. "I really wanted to pound mochi."

"And you did it. You pounded mochi. You're the first under-ten-year-old and the first girl to pound mochi in our family."

My lips twitched into an almost smile.

Sophie crossed her arms. "I wish I had thought of asking to pound mochi."

I did something that Sophie had never done. Even if she pounded mochi next year, I did it first. I was the expert!

This time my mouth turned up into a real smile.

"Come on," Sophie said, tugging my arm. "Before everyone discovers your secret hiding place."

I let Sophie lead me home.
"How did you know about
my secret hiding place?"

"I'm your big sister. I need to watch out for you."

Even though Sophie didn't play with me anymore and even though she was bossier than ever, for once, having a big sister didn't seem so bad.

We walked home, our shoulders almost touching. I went back to babysitting and Sophie went back to mochi-making with cousin Anna.

"You're home!" Cassie said. She wrapped her arms around me and squeezed.

"Yes, and I pounded mochi," I whispered to her.

MOCHi QUEEN

In the living room, I watched three DVDs, played two board games, and built a castle out of blocks with Cassie and Leo. Nobody came in to check on us. They were all busy.

For lunch, I took Cassie and Leo into the kitchen to eat the peanut butter sandwiches Mom had made that morning. Outside, everyone else kept making mochi and taking turns eating lunch.

Cassie and Leo didn't want to nap. We put

together two puzzles. I was getting tired when, finally, I heard the door open and everyone coming into the house. Mochi-tsuki was over!

After a full day of making mochi, dinner was always takeout from Romero's Pizza. Mom, the aunties, and Obaachan went straight from mochi-making into the kitchen. They had to cook the food for tomorrow's New Year's Day feast. Tomorrow, we would eat fried chicken, potato salad, sushi, beef teriyaki, and rice.

The smell of boiling potatoes for the potato salad mixed with the smell of tomato sauce and melted cheese from our dinner. Yum!

All the kids ate dinner at a folding table in

the living room, while the adults ate in the kitchen so they could watch over the cooking. I grabbed for the last slice of pepperoni pizza at the same time as Eddie. I braced myself, ready to fight him for it. To my surprise, Eddie let go.

"You can have it," he said with a shrug. "You're going to need all the energy you can get for next year."

"Next year?"

"For mochi-pounding." He snatched a slice of plain cheese pizza instead.

"I'll get to help next year?"

He didn't answer. He shoved the pizza into his huge mouth and bit off half the slice. Gross.

"You know," he said with his mouth full, "last year, I didn't even get to hit it by myself. My dad helped me."

I raised my eyebrows. I didn't know why he was telling me this.

"But," he said, spitting bits of pizza out onto the table, "I'm sure I could have done better than you if I'd been given the chance!"

I sucked in my bottom lip, but this time so I wouldn't smile. It sounded to me like Eddie was jealous!

"You're not going to eat that, then?" He eyed my pizza.

I could be nice, too. It was lukewarm by now anyway. I slid my plate over to him.

"Thanks, Jasmine Pee!" He took the slice and left for the kitchen.

"Misa-chan." Obaachan sat down next to me. It was the first time I'd talked to her since the morning.

"Hi, Obaachan. Did you get any pizza?"

She shook her head, crinkling her nose. "That not dinner! You need eat more Japanese foods."

I nodded, because she was Obaachan.

"Here." She handed me my apron, folded

neatly in a square. "For you. You wear next year when you pound mochi."

I grinned. "Really?"

"Yes. You make me proud."

I thanked her. "Arigato, Obaachan."

"You are welcome," she said.

"Jasmine Toguchi!" Mom's voice bounced into my ears.

My heart pounded like a mochi hammer. Was I in trouble?

Mom came around the corner holding a plate with the biggest mochi ever. Wowee zowee! It was toasted golden and sprinkled with cinnamon and sugar, just the way I liked it.

"Jasmine Toguchi," Mom said again as she placed the plate in front of me. "You are the Mochi Queen!"

Obaachan raised her teacup. "You strong girl!"

Everyone else came into the living room,

cheering. Even not-so-mean cousin Eddie was clapping.

"But it's not midnight yet," I said. I almost drooled smelling the sweet mochi.

"I think today we learned it's okay to break some rules," Mom said.

I waved Sophie over. She sat next to me and together we ate the first mochi of the year!

AUTHOR'S NOTE

Mochi (*moh-chee*) is a Japanese treat made from sticky rice. It usually looks like a small white ball. Sometimes it is cut into neat rectangles or squares. It is a sticky, chewy dessert that can be eaten at any time of the year, although it is especially important during the New Year's holiday celebration, or Oshogatsu (*oh-show-ga-tsoo*). According to Japanese tradition, eating mochi at the start of the year ensures good luck.

Mochi-tsuki (*moh-chee-tsoo-kee*) literally means mochi-making. Mochi-tsuki involves preparation and hard work. A day before mochi-tsuki, the special mochi rice has to be washed and soaked. The next day, the rice is steamed in big batches.

While it is still hot, the cooked rice is placed in a mortar called an usu (*oo-soo*). It can be made out of stone or wood. A special mallet or hammer called a kine (*kee-neh*) is used to pound the rice into mochi. The wooden hammer is heavy and it's very hard work to pound the rice. Traditionally, it has been considered a job for men.

To keep the rice from sticking to the mortar, another person reaches into the mortar in between pounding to wet the rice and turn it.

Once the rice is pounded into mochi, it is taken to a table that is dusted with mochiko (*moh-chee-koh*), a rice flour. The flour keeps the mochi from sticking to the table.

It is traditional for the women to form the mochi treats by pinching pieces off the hot ball of mochi and rolling them into smaller balls.

Mochi can be put in a soup of vegetables and broth called ozoni (*oh-zone-ee*) to eat on New Year's morning. Mochi can also be toasted. Some people like to eat it with sugar and soy sauce.

These days, many Japanese families no longer make their own mochi. They either buy it from stores or use special mochi-making machines (like rice cookers). Turn the page for a microwave recipe that you can use to make your own mochi at any time of the year. Enjoy!

MICROWAVE MOCHI RECIPE

ALWAYS BE SURE TO HAVE A GROWN-UP HELP YOU!

INGREDIENTS

- 1½ cups mochiko (Japanese rice flour), plus a couple of handfuls
- 1 cup granulated white sugar
- 1½ cups water
- cooking spray

Note: Mochiko can be purchased in Asian grocery stores or online.

UTENSILS

Measuring cups, medium or large bowl, mixing spoon, 9×9 square microwavable pan (glass or ceramic), cutting board, small knife

INSTRUCTIONS

1. Mix 1½ cups of mochiko with the sugar and water in a bowl until smooth.

2. Spray microwavable pan with cooking spray.

3. Pour mochiko mixture into pan.

4. Microwave on high for 7½ minutes until ingredients become a puffy dough-like mass. (Cooking times may vary.)

5. Dust cutting board with mochiko.

6. With an adult's help, remove hot pan from microwave. Flip pan over onto the mochiko-dusted cutting board. Cooked mochi should come out of the pan in one big square.

7. Let mochi cool until you can safely handle it.

8. Cut into small square pieces.

HOW TO EAT MOCHI

You can eat mochi as is, or dip it into sugar, cinnamon, and/or soy sauce for extra flavor. You can also toast it lightly in a toaster oven for a crispier outer shell. Mochi is very sticky, so take small bites and chew carefully.

HOW TO STORE MOCHI

Wrap cooled mochi loosely in wax paper and store at room temperature. Eat within two days.

DEBBI MICHIKO FLORENCE is a third-generation Japanese American, and has fond memories of sharing in her family's traditions while growing up in California. Debbi now lives in Connecticut with her husband, their two ducks, Darcy and Lizzy, and their bunny, Aki. Her favorite mochi is azuki mochi—with red-bean filling.

ELIZABET VUKOVIĆ received her B.F.A. from the Academy of Art University in San Francisco, California. She specializes in children's book illustration, but enjoys experimenting with character design, concept art, fashion illustration, and decorative art. She currently resides in Rotterdam, the Netherlands.